For Andrea & Claudia
— I.F.

For Mom & Dad, who helped
— J.T.

ISBN 0-439-26026-4

12 11 10 9 8 7 6 5 4 3 2   1 2 3 4 5 6/0

Printed in the U.S.A.   08

First Scholastic printing, January 2001

The Very Lazy Ladybug

by Isobel Finn

Illustrated by Jack Tickle

SCHOLASTIC INC.
New York Toronto London Auckland Sydney
Mexico City New Delhi Hong Kong

This is the story of
a very lazy ladybug.

She liked to sleep all day . . .

and all night.

Because she slept
all day and all night,
this lazy ladybug didn't
know how to fly.

One day the lazy
ladybug wanted to
sleep somewhere else.
But what could she do
if she couldn't fly?

Then the lazy
ladybug had a
very good idea.

she hopped into her pouch.

But the kangaroo liked to

JUMP!

"I can't sleep in here,"
cried the lazy ladybug.
"It's too bumpy."

So when a tiger padded by . . .

she hopped onto his back.

But the tiger liked to

ROAR!

"I can't sleep here,"
said the lazy ladybug.
"It's too noisy."

So when a crocodile swam by . . .

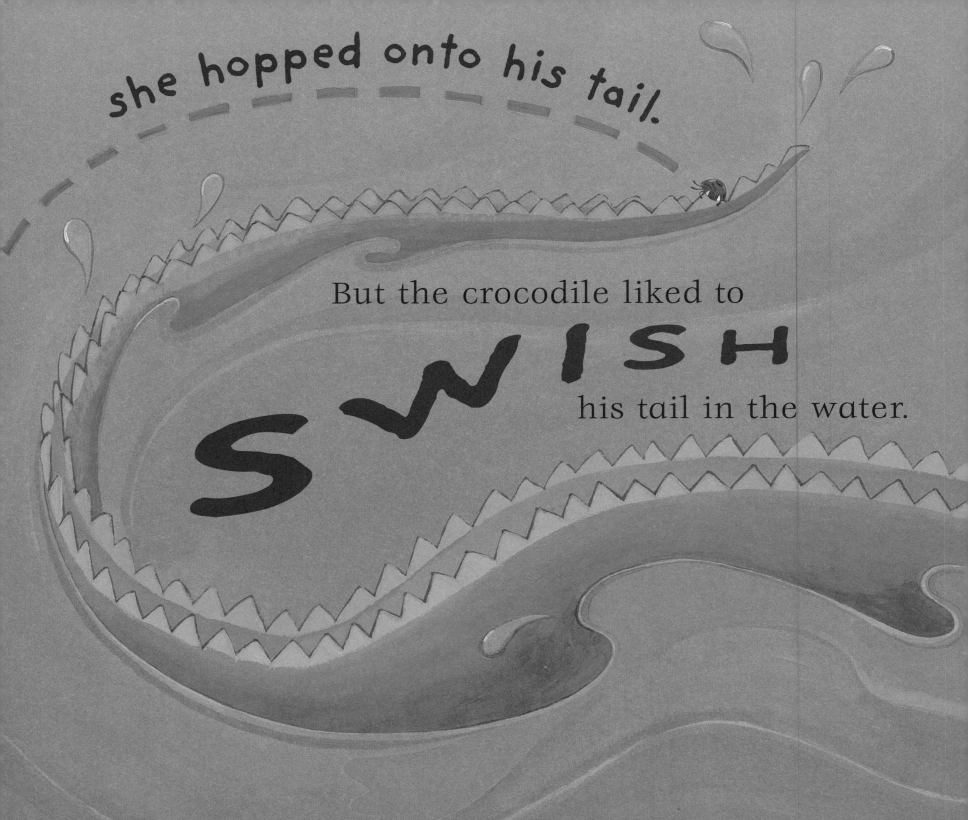

she hopped onto his tail.

But the crocodile liked to

SWISH

his tail in the water.

"I can't sleep here," said the lazy ladybug. "I'll fall into the river!"

So when a monkey swung by . . .

she hopped onto her head.

But the monkey liked to

SWING

from branch to branch.

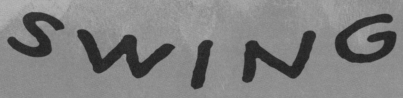

"I can't sleep here," said the lazy ladybug. "I'm feeling dizzy."

So when a bear ambled by . . .

she hopped onto his ear.

But the bear
liked to
SCRATCH!

"I can't sleep here,"
said the lazy ladybug.
"He'll never sit still."

So when a tortoise plodded by . . .

she hopped onto her shell.

But the tortoise liked to
S N O O Z E
in the sun.
"I can't sleep here,"
said the lazy ladybug.
"It's too hot."

So when an elephant walked by . . . .

she hopped onto his trunk.

"At last!" thought
the lazy ladybug.
"I've found
someone
who doesn't . . .

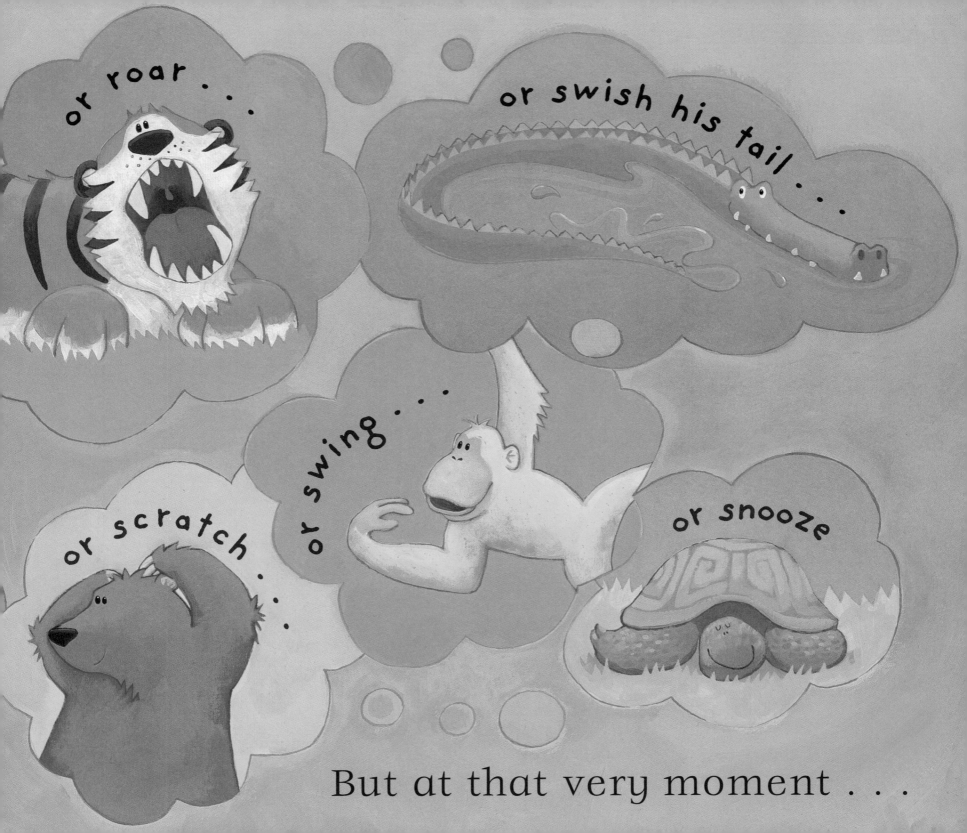

But at that very moment . . .

the elephant

had to fly at last!

HOOₒ

And poor old lazy ladybug . . .